W9-CKI-638

Bungee Hero

BY JULIE BERTAGNA
ILLUSTRATED BY BRANN GARVEY

Librarian Reviewer
Kathleen Baxter
Children's Literature Consultant
formerly with Anoka County Library, MN
BA College of Saint Catherine, St. Paul, MN
MA in Library Science, University of Minnesota

Reading Consultant
Elizabeth Stedem
Educator/Consultant, Colorado Springs, CO
MA in Elementary Education, University of Denver, CO

STONE ARCH BOOKS
Minneapolis San Diego

First published in the United States in 2007
by Stone Arch Books,
151 Good Counsel Drive, P.O. Box 669,
Mankato, Minnesota 56002.
www.stonearchbooks.com

Published by arrangement with
Barrington Stoke Ltd, Edinburgh.

Library of Congress Cataloging-in-Publication Data
Bertagna, Julie.
Bungee Hero / by J. Bertagna; illustrated by Brann Garvey.
p. cm. — (Pathway Books)
Summary: Although he finds him boring at first, Adam soon becomes fascinated with Mr. Haddock, a World War II parachutist honored as a hero, who lost his legs and now lives in the nursing home where Adam's mother works.
ISBN-13: 978-1-59889-099-0 (hardcover)
ISBN-10: 1-59889-099-9 (hardcover)
ISBN-13: 978-1-59889-253-6 (paperback)
ISBN-10: 1-59889-253-3 (paperback)
[1. Heroes—Fiction. 2. Amputees—Fiction. 3. People with disabilities—Fiction. 4. Parachuting—Fiction.] I. Garvey, Brann, ill. II. Title. III. Series.
PZ7.B4627Bun 2007
[Fic]—dc22 2006007171

Art Director: Heather Kindseth
Cover Graphic Designer: Brann Garvey
Interior Graphic Designer: Kay Fraser

1 2 3 4 5 6 11 10 09 08 07 06

Printed in the United States of America.

TABLE OF CONTENTS

CHAPTER 1

AN ANGRY HERO

Adam kicked the ball hard, and it shot past the goalie. Yes! It was in! The huge crowd rose to its feet and yelled. Adam held up his arm in triumph. He was a hero.

"Hurry up and get in the car, Adam."

"Aw, Mom," said Adam with a groan. "Do I have to?"

His daydream faded.

The crowd in the stands was gone, and so were the two soccer teams. Adam was back in his own yard. He took one last kick at his pretend ball, aiming at the living room window. Then he got in the car.

His mom had been watching him. "You'll have to pay for that smashed window," she told him.

Mom might be a pain in the neck about some things, but she could still make a joke.

"Do we have to go to that stupid old people's home today?" Adam asked. "You know all the kids go down to the food court after school on Fridays."

"They'll be fine without you for an hour," Mom told him.

"Anyway, I only need you to carry a few boxes," she added. "It'll be good for you. A soccer hero has to keep in shape."

"Not if I'm only a hero in my dreams," Adam said as they drove off to the nursing home. "I can just pretend I'm in shape."

Adam's mom worked as a helper at the nursing home. Sometimes Adam came along to help out.

Mom loved to hear the old people tell stories about their lives. But they bored Adam out of his mind.

It was even worse being there on a Friday after school when he should have been at the mall, making plans for the weekend with Nick and Grant.

At the nursing home, Adam went down to the basement and began carrying boxes of canned food up to the kitchen as his mom had asked him to do.

It took a long time. Mom still wasn't ready when he was finished.

"It won't kill you to wait a little longer, Adam," she told him. "I just want to take Mr. Haddock out for a little fresh air. He's been in bed all week with a terrible cold."

Adam looked at his watch. He was so bored that he thought waiting might just kill him. Nick and Grant would go off without him if he didn't get down to the mall soon.

Mom went to get Mr. Haddock.

Haddock is a funny name, Adam thought. Does he look like a large fish? Is he like an old haddock who tells long, boring stories about his long, boring life in the boring sea?

But Mr. Haddock was just a dull old man in a wheelchair. Adam began to kick his pretend soccer ball in front of the wheelchair as Mom pushed it along the sidewalk.

"Adam!" said Mom, as he pretended to kick the ball right over the old man's head.

Mr. Haddock looked at Adam with cold blue eyes. "If I was that boy, I'd rather pretend to play soccer than go along with an old man in a wheelchair," Mr. Haddock said. "Can we go now?"

The game in Adam's head melted away. Mom gave him an angry look. Adam walked behind Mom and Mr. Haddock without saying a word. He didn't want to risk losing his mall money.

"Mr. Haddock was in a parachute regiment in World War II, Adam," said Mom, as they walked back to the home. "He won a medal for bravery."

"So what?" Adam said. He looked at his watch again.

Nick and Grant had probably given up on him by now. The last thing Adam needed was for the old soldier to start talking about World War II.

But the old man just looked ahead with his angry eyes.

"That's just what I think," Mr. Haddock said. "Like the boy says, so what?"

Adam was shocked. He thought the old man was too deaf to hear what he said.

Mom looked really mad.

"I'm so sorry about Adam, Mr. Haddock," she said. "He wants to hurry off with his friends. And he's hungry. That's what's making him so rude."

"Ah," said Mr. Haddock.

He gave Adam another sharp look. "I see," said Mr. Haddock.

"Bye," said Adam softly, as Mom pushed the old man up the ramp and in through the door. Mr. Haddock didn't even look at him.

Funny, thought Adam. Mr. Haddock really does look a little like a fish. He had a long face and a sad mouth and those angry blue eyes. Maybe there was a fish tail under the thick blanket that was tucked around the old man. He took another look.

Then Adam got a big shock. The blanket lay flat against the leg rest of the wheelchair. The foot rest was empty, too.

Mr. Haddock couldn't have been a parachutist in World War II.

The old man had no legs.

CHAPTER 2

MR. VERTIGO

"Are you sure Mr. Haddock's not just making up a story when he says he was a war hero?" Adam asked on the way home.

Mom shook her head. "Mr. Haddock's mind is okay. And he hasn't always been an old man in a wheelchair. There are some faded photos in his room. One is of a boy about your age, with a soccer ball at his feet. I'm sure it's him," she said.

"The other picture is of a young man making a parachute landing," Mom added. "I'm sure that's him, too. He was very good looking."

Adam couldn't think of the angry old man in the wheelchair as a boy playing soccer or as young parachutist. "How did Mr. Haddock lose his legs?" Adam asked.

"I don't know," said Mom. "I don't feel comfortable asking him."

Mom stopped the car outside the mall. Nick and Grant were sitting in the food court by the window, where they could see girls walk by.

"See, they didn't go without you," said Mom. "There was no need to be rude to Mr. Haddock."

"Sorry," said Adam. He gave Mom a sweet smile. "I did carry all those boxes," he reminded her.

"You did," she said with a smile. She handed him his mall money. "But next time have a little more respect for an old man who risked his life for you."

For me? thought Adam, as he went to order a burger and a soda. It had nothing to do with me. I wasn't even born, yet.

As he waited his turn, Adam began to wonder what it was like being a war hero. What was it like to parachute from a plane and land in enemy country? To face real danger?

"Where were you?" asked Nick, when Adam finally joined them.

"There's a carnival at the park down by the river," said Nick. "Finish your burger and we'll head over there."

Grant grinned. "Mr. Vertigo's Ferris wheel is a monster. You can see it from my bedroom window."

Adam gulped down his burger. "Great. Let's go!"

* * *

The carnival was next to the river. As it grew dark, the bright lights from the rides shined in the water. The riverbank was crowded with people and noise and color.

When Adam and his friends got there, they headed straight for Mr. Vertigo's Giant Wheel.

It really is a monster, thought Adam. His heart thudded in his chest as he looked up at the seats spinning high into the night sky.

People were coming off Mr. Vertigo's Giant Wheel, still laughing and yelling. All at once, Adam knew he didn't want to go on the ride. He was afraid he would be sick. But if he chickened out, Nick and Grant would tease him about it for the rest of his life. He had to do it.

As he locked the safety bar across his seat, Adam wished he could get off, but then the ride began. The seat swayed and jerked as he swung higher and higher into the dark sky.

Adam was scared stiff.

At the top of Mr. Vertigo's Giant Wheel, Adam felt awful. He felt he was higher than the huge crane that sat on the bank of the river. He could see the edges of the city.

He was so high he felt dizzy.

Adam shut his eyes as the wheel jerked. The seat jerked wildly up and down. Then they plunged toward the ground, fast and hard.

Adam screamed.

The seat tipped forward. When Adam opened his eyes again he was racing straight down. He was going to smash into the ground!

At that moment the seat jerked back as the Ferris wheel swung it up toward the sky once more.

For a moment Adam felt better. Then he saw that he would have to do it all over again.

And again, and again, until the giant wheel finally came to a stop.

Maybe Mr. Haddock's not so boring after all, Adam thought.

When Adam got off the giant wheel, his heart was still thumping.

He had felt sick with fear. But deep inside, he had been thrilled, too.

"I did it!" Adam thought, as he raced to the bumper cars with Nick and Grant. "I really did it!"

All of a sudden he pictured Mr. Haddock not as an angry old man in a wheelchair but as a young parachutist. He saw him dropping out of the sky and crashing to earth.

Had Mr. Haddock felt the same strange mix of thrill and fear that Adam felt as he fell out of the sky on Mr. Vertigo's Giant Wheel?

CHAPTER 3

THE WAR DIARY

Adam thought about Mr. Haddock all week long. He didn't know why, but as the week went on he played less and less pretend soccer. Adam began to see himself as a World War II parachutist, dropping into enemy country.

"You don't need to come with me to the nursing home today, Adam," Mom told him on Friday afternoon. "You go and enjoy yourself."

"Oh," said Adam.

Mom looked at him. "What's the matter?"

"Nothing," said Adam. "It's just that I was planning to take Mr. Haddock out for a walk."

"Mr. Haddock!" cried Mom. "Why him? You didn't get along with him very well last week."

"What do you mean?" asked Adam.

"Oh come on, Adam," said Mom. "What are you up to?"

"Nothing," Adam told her. He added, "It's just that we're studying World War II in school and I want to ask him something."

Mom nodded.

"Oh, homework. Why didn't you say so?" Mom asked. "Well, make sure you're polite to him this time."

Adam grinned. "I'll be very nice," he said.

* * *

Mr. Haddock wasn't in the mood for a visit from Adam.

"What do you want?" he grumbled when Adam knocked on his door and asked if he'd like some fresh air. "Did your mother give you extra allowance money to visit me?"

"No," said Adam.

Could this crabby old man have ever been a brave, young war hero? I was stupid to expect Mr. Haddock to understand, Adam thought.

Adam was glad to be behind the wheelchair where he could escape Mr. Haddock's angry looks. He pushed the old man along the sidewalk. Why did he bother to come?

All of a sudden, Mr. Haddock asked, "Why would a young fellow like you want to push a grumpy old man around when he could be off with his friends?"

How did he know what Adam was thinking?

"I don't know," said Adam. "I just wanted to ask you about the war."

"Ah," said Mr. Haddock. "Homework, is it?"

"Yes . . . I mean no . . . I mean," Adam stammered.

What was it he wanted to ask? "You see, I was on Mr. Vertigo's Ferris wheel last week, at the carnival, with my friends. It was so . . ."

Adam stopped. He didn't want to admit to a war hero how scared he had been on a carnival ride.

"It was amazing," Adam went on. "And I thought it must be kind of like a parachute jump."

"So you want to know what it's like doing a parachute jump, eh?" asked Mr. Haddock. "Well, I've never been on a Ferris wheel. But getting ready to jump from a plane as you fly over enemy country is like getting ready to die. It's no carnival ride, I can tell you that. You don't risk your life on a ride, do you?"

"No," said Adam, feeling ashamed for asking.

The old man was awful. Adam turned the wheelchair around and pushed it back to the home as quickly as he could. He parked Mr. Haddock in front of the TV without saying a word, and went to wait by the car for his mom.

He should never have come. It had been a waste of time.

* * *

At breakfast one morning a few days later, Adam's mom handed him a package that had arrived in the mail for him.

"Who sent you a present?" asked his dad.

"Don't know," said Adam as he tore it open.

Inside the wrapping paper was a brown leather notebook.

PLEASE RETURN TO E. HADDOCK, said a note stuck on the front.

Adam looked inside. The pages were yellow with age and were covered with tiny writing.

Dust rose from the pages as he flipped through them.

"Adam!" Mom flapped her hand in front of her face. "You're getting dust in my cornflakes."

Adam stopped at one page and read:

May 17th 1944 2200 hours

Just about to leave on my third trip over France. We have to map out where the enemy troops are in the north.

We'll be in more danger than ever tonight. So far we've just had to dodge some sniper fire.

But we'll get the anti-aircraft gunners tonight.

I hope I live to see tomorrow.

** * **

0800 hours

Back in one piece! I would kill for a stack of pancakes and a side of bacon.

* * *

The words in the next entry were hard to read:

Jack's plane didn't make it back. My best buddy. I still feel like he's going to walk in the door any moment, yelling for his breakfast. Will he?

* * *

"Time for school, Adam, and you haven't eaten yet," said Mom.

"So what's this great book you got?" asked Dad. "It must be pretty interesting to keep you from eating breakfast."

Adam felt dazed.

"It's from Mr. Haddock," he said. "He sent me his war diary."

CHAPTER 4

DROP ZONE DISASTER

Adam put Mr. Haddock's war diary in his school backpack, but it was break time before he could look at it again. In the schoolyard he flipped through the dusty pages, trying to find the part he had read at breakfast.

What had happened to Jack, Mr. Haddock's best buddy? Did he get back safely? Was his plane shot down?

Adam hadn't been able to think about anything else all morning.

Mr. Haddock's writing was hard to read, and Adam couldn't remember the date on the page he read at breakfast.

When the bell rang at the end of break, Adam still hadn't found out what had happened to Jack.

It took Adam half of his lunch time to find the right page. Jack's plane had been shot down over France by anti-aircraft gunners before the soldiers could jump out.

He never came back. Mr. Haddock lost his best buddy.

Adam showed Nick the war diary and told him all about it.

"One day you're best friends and the next day one of you is dead," said Nick. "How weird."

The two boys looked at each other for a moment. How awful it must have been.

Adam wasn't sure if he wanted to read any more of the diary. He liked playing war games on his computer, but Mr. Haddock's diary wasn't a game. It was real. It hurt to read it.

Adam took the diary up to his room after dinner that evening. He started to read it from the beginning. He read about the hard training Mr. Haddock had to become a parachutist. He read about his night trips flying over France.

Once again he read about his friend Jack's death.

It seemed Mr. Haddock had no time to think about his friend's death before he was sent off on a new mission.

* * *

May 24th, 1944

"You don't get to be a war hero because you kill the enemy," our mission leader said tonight. "And being scared doesn't mean that you are a coward. What makes you a hero is that you set others free."

But I don't want to be a hero anymore. I thought I did. Both Jack and I did.

Now he's dead and tonight I'd give anything to get back to my old life, with my best buddy.

The lives of so many people depend on this mission. Hitler's armies are on the move across France and we must help the Resistance forces in their fight against them.

Tonight I must parachute into enemy country. I've had plenty of practice jumps, but this will be the real thing. The plane lights will switch off as we reach our drop zone. I will take my place and get ready to jump out of the plane. Below me will be black, empty space.

When we spot the signal — the single beam of a light shining in a field — we have to jump. I'll fall into thin air. I can only pray that I make a safe landing, and that the enemy is not waiting for me down below.

I'm sick with fear. But I must do it. The mission must succeed. I will do it for Jack.

The next page was blank. It seemed to be the end of the diary. Then Adam found one more entry a few pages on.

* * *

The war is now over. And today I found this old diary again. I could hardly bear to read it. This will be my last entry. I don't know why I'm writing it. Who will ever read this diary but me?

That night of the mission, we flew over the drop zone, but there was no signal. We thought that they forgot to come.

We didn't want to think they might have been taken prisoner or killed. But I had papers to give to the Resistance. I had to make the jump.

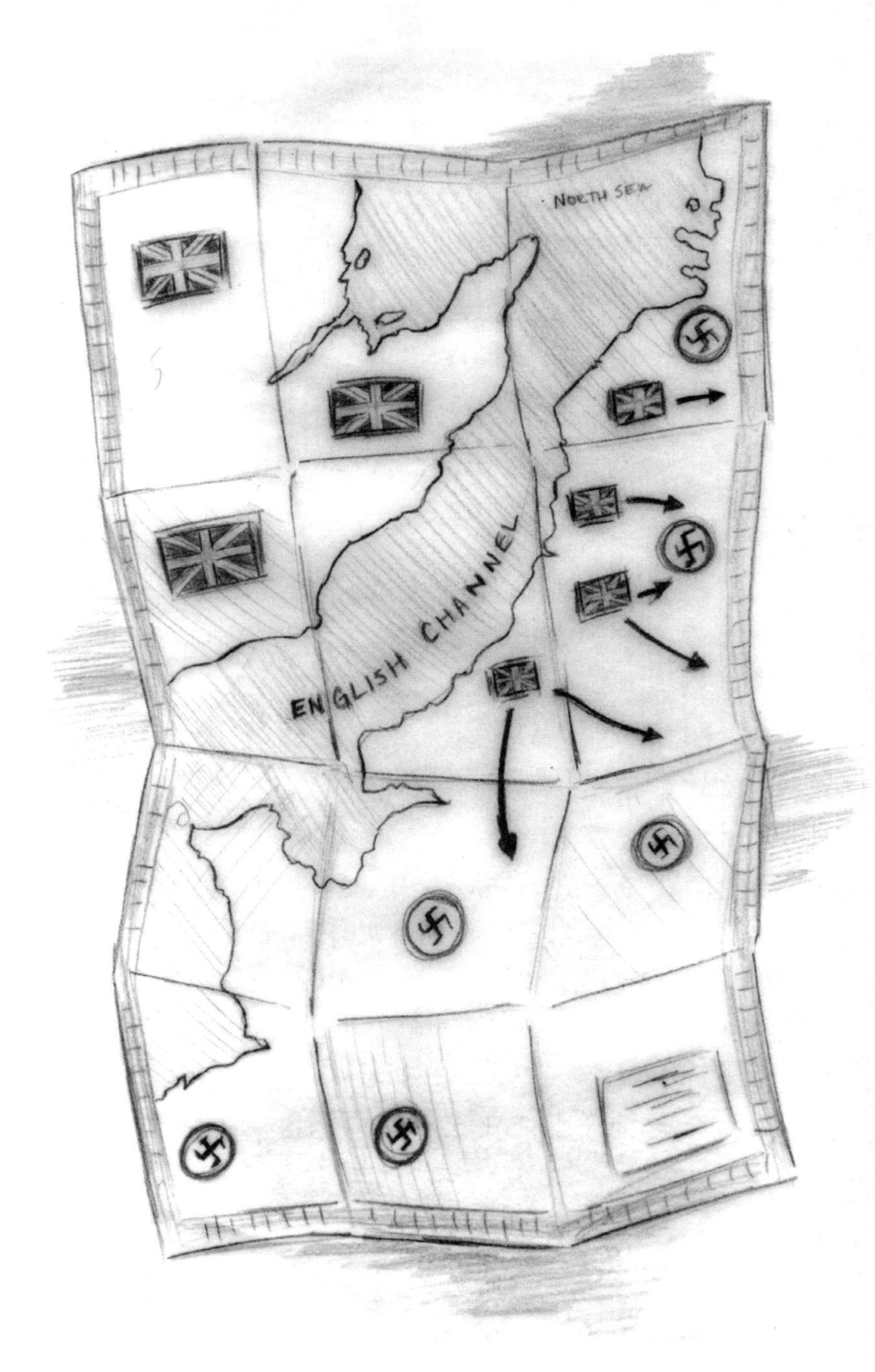
NORTH SEA
ENGLISH CHANNEL

I will never forget the moment I fell out of the plane into the icy wind. It was sheer terror! There was a great jolt as my parachute opened. Then there was the most amazing feeling as I floated down.

It was the feeling of being truly alive. "I did it!" I told myself as I crashed to earth.

A moment later the world exploded in my face.

It wasn't the drop zone. It was the wrong field. I had landed in a minefield.

I woke up days later in terrible pain in a strange bed. They told me I'd lost my legs in the blast. I wished I was dead. I had failed. I was no hero.

But they told me I was a hero. The papers I had strapped to my chest were still there when the Resistance found me. They used them to save many lives. All those lives must be worth the loss of one man's legs.

I lost my freedom so that others could be free.

Adam shut the diary. He felt odd. Then he had an amazing idea.

It felt like his mission. The mission of his life.

CHAPTER 5

MISSION BUNGEE

"A parachute jump?" said Nick. "Are you out of your mind?"

Nick and Grant stared at Adam, in shock.

"How can you do a parachute jump when you were so scared on the Ferris wheel?" asked Grant. "I saw you."

"I was not!" Adam lied. "And I didn't chicken out, did I?"

"How do you get to do a parachute jump?" asked Nick.

"I don't have a clue," Adam said. "Any ideas?"

Grant looked blank.

Nick gave a shrug.

"Look it up in the telephone book?" said Adam.

* * *

The first number Adam called almost stopped his mission in life before it began.

"Sorry, son. You have to be sixteen or older to do a parachute jump," the man on the phone told him.

Adam groaned. "The mission's off," he told the others.

"A mission, is it?" said the voice on the phone. "Does it have to be a parachute jump?"

"Yeah," said Adam.

"Too bad," said the man, "because there's always bungee jumping."

"A bungee jump!" yelled Adam. He was so excited he nearly dropped the phone. "That'll do it. I'll make it Mission Bungee!"

* * *

"Your mom will go crazy," said Adam's dad when he heard about Mission Bungee. "You'd better forget it, Adam."

"But it's for a good cause, Dad," Adam said.

"Even if it is, I just don't like the idea of it and neither will your mom," said his dad.

Adam's mom didn't go crazy. She just said no.

Adam was about to storm up to his room when he had a better idea. He picked up Mr. Haddock's war diary.

"Listen to this," he said.

He read the part about Jack and the entry written the night before Mr. Haddock's parachute jump. Then he read the last entry of all.

"Fifty years in a wheelchair," said Dad. "There must be many other men like Mr. Haddock who are spending the rest of their lives in hospitals and nursing homes," Dad added.

"It's very sad," said Mom. "But I don't see why Adam should risk his life in a bungee jump."

"I'm not risking my life," Adam said. "I'll have a safety harness and helmet. The experts will be there to make sure I'm okay."

"But why?" Mom wanted to know.

"I want to do this jump to get sponsors to donate money for an electric wheelchair. Mr. Haddock can't wheel himself around anymore. It'll give him more freedom. He deserves that."

Adam remembered the words in Mr. Haddock's diary. How the thrill of the parachute jump was the feeling of being truly alive.

"I really want to do it," Adam told his parents.

"All right," said Mom at last. "If you can prove to me it's safe, you can do it."

Then his Mom stared at him and said, "But don't come crying to me if you break your neck!"

* * *

I'm going to be sick, Adam thought.

"Ready?" asked the bungee instructor.

Adam was in a panic.

He would never be ready.

This was a crazy idea.

A very bad, crazy idea.

He no longer cared if he chickened out and made a fool of himself in front of Mom and Dad, Nick and Grant, the newspaper reporters, and all the kids and teachers from school.

He was too scared to care.

He just could not do it.

Mission Bungee, however, had become famous.

"Do it somewhere odd," the instructor had said, "so that you'll get a big crowd. The more people you get, the more money you'll raise."

So Adam chose the huge crane down by the river, the one he had seen from the top of the Ferris wheel that night at the carnival.

The bungee instructors checked it out and said it was perfect.

Now Adam was standing on top of the crane in front of a huge crowd, about to do a bungee jump.

Adam looked across at the giant wheel on the other side of the river.

Mr. Haddock was right. A ride on that was a joke compared to this.

Yet even a bungee jump couldn't be as scary as a parachute jump, one that landed you in enemy territory, right on top of an exploding mine.

You didn't even hit the ground in a bungee jump. You just landed upside down in midair at the end of an elastic safety rope.

I'll die of fear, thought Adam.

Then he saw Mr. Haddock in his wheelchair next to Mom and Dad.

When he had told Mr. Haddock about the bungee jump and why he was doing it, the old man's angry eyes had filled with tears.

Then they'd had a long talk.

Now, as Adam looked down, the old man saluted him.

Adam got ready to jump.

He could chicken out in front of everyone else, but he could not let Mr. Haddock down.

What was it Mr. Haddock's mission leader had said in the war diary? Being scared doesn't make you a coward. But giving freedom to someone else makes you a hero.

Adam shut his eyes. He counted to three.

Then he let himself fall.

ABOUT THE AUTHOR

Julie Bertagna has been dreaming up stories all her life, but she thought an ordinary girl from Scotland could never become an author. After college she was a magazine editor, then a teacher and part-time writer. She finally found out that she was wrong about being ordinary. "Whatever your dream is," she says, "work hard, don't give up, and you can make it come true."

ABOUT THE ILLUSTRATOR

Brann Garvey grew up in the great state of Iowa, where he studied art and visual communications. He graduated from the Minneapolis College of Art & Design with a degree in illustration. Brann is usually found with one or more of the following: a pencil in his hand, a comic book, a remote for watching DVDs, or his pet kitty, Iggy. When the weather is nice, Brann likes to play disc golf, and he proudly points out that Iowa is one of the world's centers for the sport. Iggy does not play.

GLOSSARY

anti-aircraft (ANT-eye-AIR-kraft)—weapons used to fight enemy planes

haddock (HAD-ock)—a cold water fish

minefield (MINE-feeld)—an area planted with exploding devices

parachute (PAIR-uh-shoot)—a strong cloth attached to ropes, used to drop people safely from planes

parachutist (PAIR-uh-shoot-ist)—a soldier trained to parachute from a plane and land in enemy territory

regiment (REJ-uh-munt)—a large group of soldiers who work together

Resistance (ri-ZISS-tuhnss)—in World War II, a secret group that worked against invading forces

sniper (SNYE-puhr)—one who hides to shoot enemy soldiers

vertigo (VUR-tuh-go)—a feeling of dizziness

DISCUSSION QUESTIONS

1. Adam thinks old people are boring. Do you think so, too? Why or why not?

2. Nick and Grant saw that Adam was scared on Mr. Vertigo's Big Wheel. Have you ever been afraid to go on a new ride in front of your friends? Did you try it or not? What was it like?

3. In what ways is Adam's bungee jump like Mr. Haddock's parachute drop? In what ways is it different?

WRITING PROMPTS

1. Pretend you are a soldier and your best friend is missing. Write a diary entry describing your feelings.

2. Now pretend you're a newspaper reporter. Write a news story about the missing soldier – just the facts of who, what, and when. Which one did you like writing better, the diary entry or the news report? Why?

3. Adam decides to raise money for an electric wheelchair for Mr. Haddock. How did he get sponsors? Write a sheet that Adam could give to people, telling about Mission Bungee and asking them to donate money.

ALSO PUBLISHED BY STONE ARCH BOOKS

On the Run
by H. Townson

Ronnie hates sports. When he pretends to be sick so he can get out of Sports Day, he encounters something much scarier than the high jump.

The House With No Name
by P. Goodhart

When Jamie moves into a new house, he senses something strange. His dad has an accident, and it's up to Jamie to solve the house's secret mystery.

Dead Cool
by Peter Clover

Sammy gets more than he bargained for when he brings home his new parrot, Polly. It turns out some of Polly's pirate friends are along for the ride.

Biker City
Anthony Masters

Todd lives in a dangerous desert wasteland where water is scarce. Gangs of outlaw bikers rule the region. Todd's dad has disappeared, so it's up to Todd to face the Bikers on his own.

INTERNET SITES

Do you want to know more about subjects related to this book? Or are you interested in learning about other topics? Then check out FactHound, a fun, easy way to find Internet sites.

Our investigative staff has already sniffed out great sites for you!

Here's how to use FactHound:

1. Visit *www.facthound.com*
2. Select your grade level.
3. To learn more about subjects related to this book, type in the book's ISBN number: **1598890999**.
4. Click the **Fetch It** button.

FactHound will fetch the best Internet sites for you!